For Briony and Simon
A.M.

For John and Alexander
P.L.

First published 1987
by Walker Books Ltd
184-192 Drummond Street
London NW1 3HP

Text © 1987 Adrian Mitchell
Illustrations © 1987 Priscilla Lamont

First printed 1987
Printed and bound by L.E.G.O., Vicenza, Italy

British Library Cataloguing in Publication Data
Mitchell, Adrian
Our mammoth goes to school. – (Our mammoth)
I. Title   II. Lamont, Priscilla
823'.914[J] PZ7

ISBN 0-7445-0739-1

Our Mammoth
Goes to School

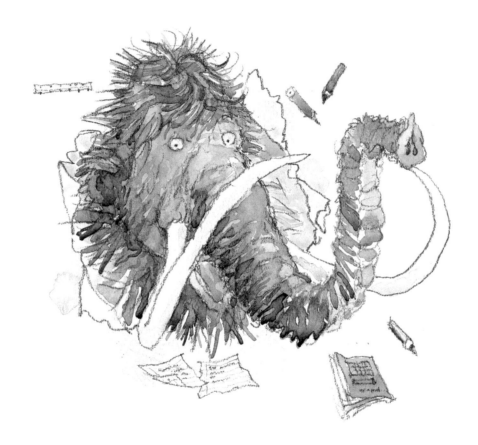

Written by
Adrian Mitchell

Illustrated by
Priscilla Lamont

WALKER BOOKS
LONDON

We are the Gumble Twins,
Bing and Saturday Gumble.
We have a book called

How to Look After Your Mammoth.

It says, "Mammoths are clever.
Mammoths like to learn."
So our Mum, Sally Gumble, said,
"Better take Buttercup to school."

We rode Buttercup into
the playground.
All the children cheered.
Out came both our teachers.
We have a good funny teacher
called Lucy Moose.
Lucy Moose fetched Buttercup
a bucket of milk.

We have a bad sad teacher
    called Mr Binko.
Mr Binko frowned and said,
"No mammoths allowed in my school."
Lucy Moose smiled and said,
"We'll have our history lesson
    out in the playground."

She told us a story of the old days
    when there were
    hundreds of mammoths.
At playtime we all used Buttercup
    as a climbing frame.
We used her curving tusks for slides.
Buttercup purred like a motorboat.

Mr Binko stared and said,
"That mammoth has fleas.
    They are big as sparrows
    but not as pretty."
Saturday said, "They are only
    mammoth fleas.
    They won't itch people."

Bing said, "She only has four fleas.
    We call them Whizzby, Fizzby,
    Thisbe and Chips."
We said, "All mammoths have fleas.
    They are fond of their fleas.
    A mammoth with no fleas is lonely."

Mr Binko grinned and said,
"Everybody ready for the School Trip?
Today we're going to Animal Park.
But we're not taking Buttercup
or Bing or Saturday Gumble
because of those dirty fleas."

Lucy Moose said, "Sorry,
    you'd better go home."
We climbed up on to Buttercup's back.
But when the school bus drove away
    Buttercup started to follow it.
Have you ever been for
    a wild mammoth ride?

We shouted out, "Stop!"
But nothing would stop her.
We hung on tight to the hair on
    the hump behind her head.
        She went bumping along,
        faster and faster,
        past bikes, past cars.

First she went
Gerlumpergumper.

Then she went
Lottentotten,
Lottentotten.

Then she went
Snoppitter
Poppitter
Snoppitter
Poppitter.

Then she went Ballooby Ballooby
Ballooby Ballooby Ballooby Ballooby
all the way to Animal Park.

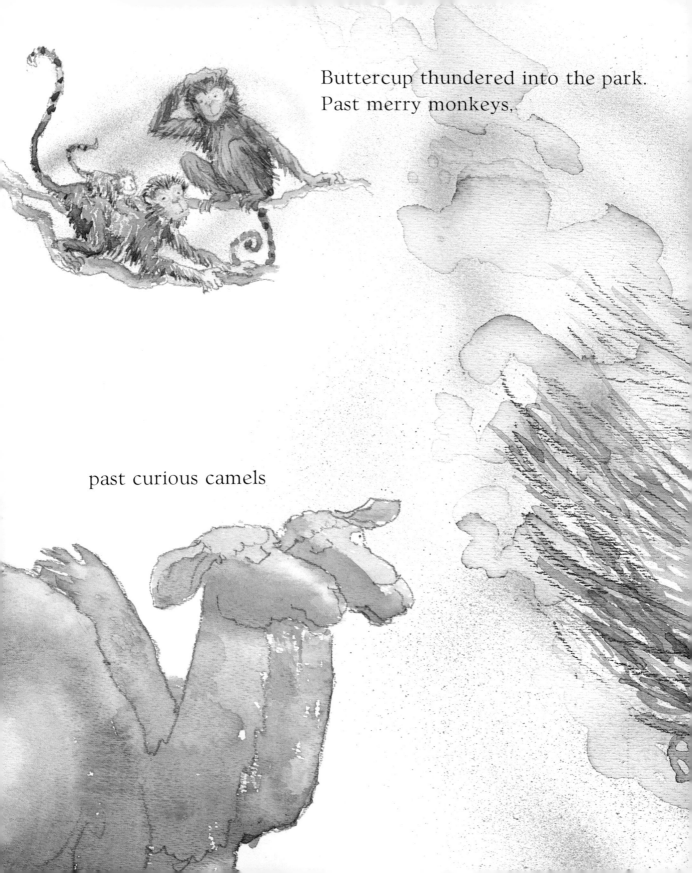

Buttercup thundered into the park.
Past merry monkeys,

past curious camels

past terrible tigers

past zigzag zebras.

Buttercup slowed down beside a field.
There were eight elephants eating hay.
Buttercup lifted up her trunk
   and made a sound like
   a big brass band.
All the elephants came to meet her
   blowing on their trumpets.
The elephants crowded
   round Buttercup.
They sniffed her.
They patted her.
They gazed into her
   brown and golden eyes.
They all made a noise
   that sounded like "Yes".
Then they led Buttercup
   down to a lake.

Buttercup and the elephants
    sploshed into the water.
They played Fountains.
They played Underwater
    Hide-and-Seek.
They played Musical Mudbaths.
We played too and got
    wet as walruses.
But we didn't mind.

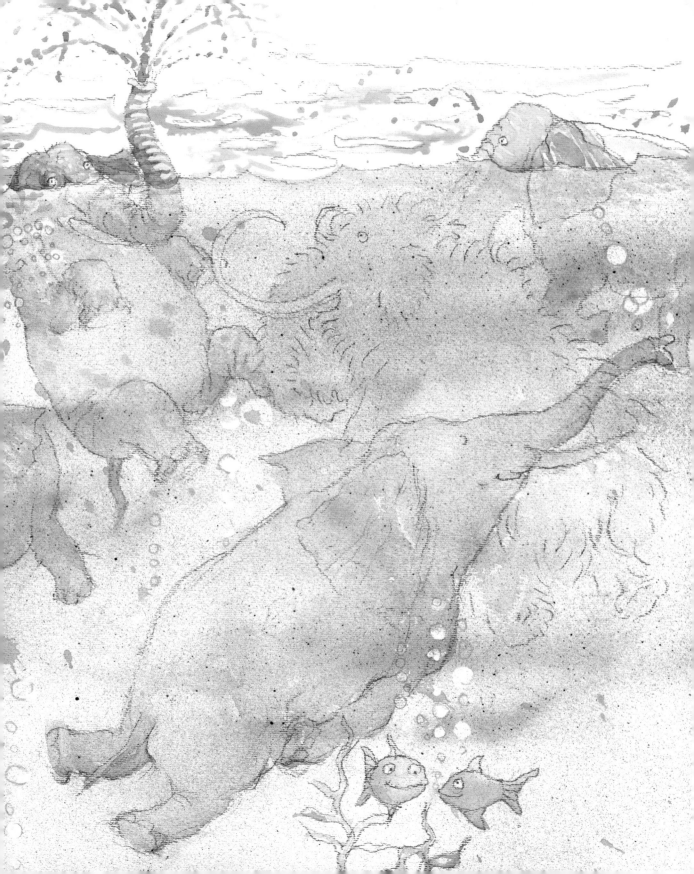

Then the School Trip found us.
Lucy Moose gave Buttercup
   a bunch of dandelions.
But Mr Binko laughed at Buttercup.
"Great hairy monster with fleas," he said.
He laughed so much his wig
   fell in a puddle.

We picked up his wig and
   handed it back.
We nearly burst,
   but we didn't laugh.
But Buttercup shook and
   snuffled a bit
   and so did Lucy Moose.

When we got home we told our Mum.
She promised to take Buttercup
    every Sunday to visit
    her friends in Animal Park.
We had beans for supper.
Buttercup had six buckets of soup.
Her fleas had tomato juice.
Then we went to bed
    and we slept like beanbags.